A Day in Eternity

T. Herman

Order this book online at www.trafford.com/08-1286
or email orders@trafford.com

Most Trafford titles are also available at major online book retailers.

Note for Librarians: A cataloguing record for this book is available from Library
and Archives Canada at www.collectionscanada.ca/amicus/index-e.html

Printed in Victoria, BC, Canada.

ISBN: 978-1-4251-8794-1

*We at Trafford believe that it is the responsibility of us all, as both individuals
and corporations, to make choices that are environmentally and socially sound.
You, in turn, are supporting this responsible conduct each time you purchase a
Trafford book, or make use of our publishing services. To find out how you are
helping, please visit www.trafford.com/responsiblepublishing.html*

*Our mission is to efficiently provide the world's finest, most comprehensive
book publishing service, enabling every author to experience success.
To find out how to publish your book, your way, and have it available
worldwide, visit us online at www.trafford.com/10510*

www.trafford.com

North America & international
toll-free: 1 888 232 4444 (USA & Canada)
phone: 250 383 6864 ♦ fax: 250 383 6804
email: info@trafford.com

The United Kingdom & Europe
phone: +44 (0)1865 487 395 ♦ local rate: 0845 230 9601
facsimile: +44 (0)1865 481 507 ♦ email: info.uk@trafford.com

10 9 8 7 6 5 4 3

To all parents…

…because sometimes we need fairy tales too.

Dedicated to my mother.

So many thanks to my two wonderful daughters.

BERNIE,

I VALUE YOUR CONVERSATION
AND APPRECIATE YOUR FRIENDSHIP.

THANKS FOR YOUR INTEREST
IN MY STORY.

Prologue

Once there was a young world with young gods; and in this world the gods placed beings of all sizes and shapes. Beings much like us shared this world with the likes of elves, dwarves, and countless other races.

Many of these creatures learned such arts as magic, nature, combat, and a few even worshiped the little understood gods.

Destiny and freewill were two strings the gods used to create hope and hardship for all of these creatures; most of whom were quite unaware or unconcerned with the gods and their strings.

Following is but a small piece of one such creature's story.

1) Twilight

Some men resist the strings attached to them; some do not. But all would agree it is better to have ties to the gods than not; and if those strings have led them to here and now, then so be it.

The ocean is vast and unforgiving. Those who dare challenge it are either brave or foolish. It is often difficult to separate bravery from foolishness when it comes to men with a purpose. But today the men of the warship *Talon* are cutting through the sea at full sail. Topside, the crew is using every bone and muscle to keep her on course and at full speed. This ship is in a hurry. Below deck are those not of the crew. Although passengers, they too are with purpose and are preparing for something... something big.

Odd at first glance, yet clearly one with the others, is a well kept woman. She appears most capable in helping others put on their armor, stow their weapons, and make peace with their god.

This young woman's name is Lia. She is neatly dressed with no armor or weapon, and she is preparing bandages. It isn't long before an observer would notice the emotional and physical distance the entire team keeps from Lia.

That is all but one - Kemendil.

The group is part of a master plan and these two cannot allow any distraction. However, Lia has been with this group only a few weeks and has developed a strong friendship with Kemendil. Nevertheless, Kemendil could not resist the desire to learn more of this mysterious woman and the two have maintained a careful association. Both will admit the relationship is odd, yet both will admit it's undeniably strong. The wise ones of the party call Kemendil a fool. The unknowing are envious of him. Lia knows this relationship with Kemendil will only make things much worse later for both of them.

This bond is neither romantic nor practical. It does, however, demand commitment and sacrifice. The two have neither stopped to ponder the situation nor have they sought to avoid it. They have, however, managed to establish an understanding, or at the very least, an appreciation for the burden the other carries. Such mutual respect is very rare and often unrealized in any relationship.

Marvros, the leader of this band of heroes, orders his men topside. Archers place arrows about the deck, sword masters become one with the arena, and the healers pray. Each man focuses on his part of what lays ahead, yet not one doubts or asks why.

Lia observes the masters.

She is keenly aware of each man; his equipment, his position, and his soul...for Lia sees into their hearts. Knowing before they do what each is capable of and will accomplish. This ability of hers is not a skill, but rather an ability. It's a connection with the others that bonds her to them. Not unlike her bond with Kemendil. Some of the men fear it. Some embrace it. All accept that its presence makes them stronger, and not one would want to be without it right now.

The ocean is loud; the ship groans due to the stress under which it has been placed. The wind in the *Talon*'s sails screams; yet the deck, with all of its men, is eerily calm. Destiny or freewill, call it what you choose, brings focus to the mind and peace to the heart.

2) Nightfall

Marvros is one creature to which the gods have firmly attached their strings. Those who have the gods' attention generally consider themselves either blessed or cursed. Marvros does not consider himself blessed.

Marvros is the reason this ship, crew, and battle party are here, now, and in the middle of the ocean; and the gods are the reason for Marvros. He looks far off the stern of the ship. The grey horizon appears to be an eternity away, but Marvros knows his destiny is not measured in miles. He cannot look away for too long for soon his destiny will be upon him.

Preparation is the weapon against fear, and Marvros has prepared well. He turns his gaze away from the 'future' and looks upon the 'now'. He walks over to the rail and watches over the deck of the *Talon* as the activity of his preparedness settles. Unavoidably, everyone is watching everyone else. It's not distrust or uncertainty, just a settling gaze from one hero to another. They take the time now to recognize the commitment and sacrifice of the other, because it was not appropriate to discuss such things earlier, and because most likely they will not be around to do it later.

These men did not exist before The Calling. Most of their lives were without hope and meaning. The barbarians of the land determine one's worthiness by the strength of their enemies. Even barbarians would fear to think too much about the pending enemy that awaits this band. Duty is a double-edged sword. Without it, one may avoid suffering but also be without purpose. There is no choice for the chosen and no denying The Calling.

The enemy is a ship with no name. Behind them, as if dropped from the sky, this monstrous black vessel is within minutes of reaching them. Those who speak of it fear to place a name on something so terrifying. It is hoped that without a name, then perhaps it does not exist.

Name or not, this flotilla of death is real and clearly has business with Marvros. It slices through the water as though thrust by a hurricane. It is said to be a shell for the unnatural; a vessel for lost souls. One thing known for certain is that its only purpose is to take revenge on the living. The *Talon* crew courageously keeps their ship on its doomed course.

Marvros's men prepare and take their positions as the death ship looms.

The cold of death and disease reaches them first, as if a test of their courage. It hangs like a wet blanket on a winter's night. Alone, just this sense of evil would break the best; but these men are more than the best...they are heroes. Heroes such as these have been 'here' before...not a place; not even a time. 'Here', is a sacrifice. Standing up for what is right and doing what has to be done is what separates a hero from the rest.

Just as the black ship is about to go starboard the crew cuts the rigging, tacks the sails, and brings the *Talon* hard to starboard, cutting the black ship off and putting her on the *Talon*'s port side. With the death ship caught unprepared for a port attack, the *Talon* unleashes its ballistae and draws first blood. The *Talon*'s heavy bolts pierce clean through the black ship's decrepit hull, taking some of the accursed bodies into the water with them. This ship of death is nothing more than a past sunken wreck kept afloat by some unnatural means.

Whatever power is at work here is not known, nor can be explained by any man.

The screaming and wailing from the death ship is unnerving. It is not the sounds of suffering from the attack but instead the sounds of rage and terror.

'Animated corpses' is the only way to describe the beings on deck. The battle is swift. Charging across ropes and grapples, the invading force soon brings the battle to the deck of the *Talon*. Dead or not, the vile creatures of the dark ship cut and break like the living. The men on this mission knew it could be a one-way trip. Lia and the men of the *Talon* charge the death ship with ropes and hooks of their own.

Suicide mission or not, victory does not lie in defeating the creatures on the deck. This team knows it has to destroy the source to win, and to do that they must take the battle below deck of the black ship...deep into the bowels of death and decay. Marvros' men are truly brave and cunning. Their skill keeps them alive, and their courage gains them ground. Success is not without price, and duty demands sacrifice. Without hesitation, each man intercepts a charge to protect and allow Marvros to advance toward his goal. Each according to their own ability heals, rearms, and protects the other. Good must triumph at all costs.

The undead realize too late that the real battle is about to take place below. They pursue the heroes and catch them in the presence of It. This master of death is an abomination of bones and flesh that has been drawn together in a perverted mass of body and limbs that reach seemingly forever in all directions. Bridges of electricity jump from its flesh to its minions, giving them energy and purpose. One of Marvros' men slashes a limb of the Death Lord and all can feel the black ship jolt. Marvros draws the wretched lord's attention by releasing magical energy of his own into the cursed body mass. His archers distract the underlings while the swordsmen hold off the returning undead boarding party.

Both good and evil give the ultimate sacrifice for their own particular greater cause. 'Righteous', when you agree with the cause; 'fanatic', when you do not. The decks roar as the unstoppable meet the immoveable and the ship tosses from side to side. Energy and smoke fill the air. It is difficult to see far and impossible to know what is happening. What is certain is that both the Death Lord and Marvros are still alive; evident by the death ship still afloat, yet violently rocking.

This time, the gods favor the might and sacrifice of the heroes over that of the cursed behemoth and it falls; and in that instant, so do all its undead spawn. Bulkheads and supports snap like twigs having lost the only energy holding it together. The black ship begins to list hard and fast. Orders can be heard to retreat to the *Talon*. Lia and the surviving heroes emerge from the wretched gas and smoke carrying some of the fallen; as the death ship returns to the deep dark grave from which it came.

3) Night

Shear force of will is all that keeps alive what's left of the crew and of Marvros' men. The dead have been cared for and the casualties tended to. The *Talon* is heavily damaged but afloat. Able bodies make the best of the wreckage and help their ship make her way home. Beaten and exhausted, resting or repairing the ship, all aboard occasionally break away to cast a glimpse of Lia. Tending to the last of the injured, Lia puts away her things and remains looking down.

The next few hours will be an eternity for her, and she delays its beginning. Her heart is heavy, for it is time to say goodbye to an old friend. Waiting for her attention is Marvros' body, carried from the black ship by her and the men. It lies under a cover and has been left alone. Most of the survivors have been traveling with Marvros long enough to learn of the legend; some hearing more of the tale than others. Regardless, each has a strong opinion and they tend to divide.

"Damn the gods who find entertainment in the manipulation of man. Why me? I did not ask for this. I do not want this burden. You are not giving me something; you are instead taking something away." Yet, try as they may, they cannot run, deny, or hide from The Calling. Lia finds most men in this camp. Marvros was one. And although he did not embrace his calling to be a hero he did have the unmistakable trait all heroes posses...complete and unconditional self sacrifice.

Then there are some who view The Calling as a blessing; a sign that they are worthy of the attention of a greater being. Glory and recognition will befall them and commoners will admire them. Often lost in the moment, these heroes can overlook the small needs of another. Heroes are still mortals and seek simplicity.   They carelessly force something so grand and obscure, such as destiny, into limited black and white.

Although sometimes weak, the hero's heart always comes through in the end. Knowing all heroes are only men, Lia looks beyond these petty shortcomings and draws strength from the heroes' will and courage to grow and be great. This strength, together with her infinite wisdom, instills in her great patience; a patience often gone unrecognized or taken for granted by most heroes.

From onlookers on the deck of the *Talon*, a conflicting mix of resentment and admiration hang in the heavy air as Lia stands and turns toward Marvros. This is not her first walk, nor is it likely to be her last. This is Lia's walk of forgiveness. This is her time; her way of asking for forgiveness from the survivors, the fallen, and The One. Asking for forgiveness is not to be confused with shame. She does not regret the actions she has taken, but by acknowledging this moment, Lia allows the others to reconcile with themselves, with each other, and with her.

She holds Marvros firmly and with care. The attention she gives his body is like a mother with her child. Every move is like a ceremony and each gesture is given with respectful. His limbs, his hair, his face; all put as if they were embracing. Then, she is still. Oddly still; and still for a long time. Uncomfortably long for the others. What is observed by onlookers is a long embrace. What actually happens is a wonderfully shared experience between Lia and the chosen one; something impossible for the others to comprehend.

Sometimes with strings come favors. Sometimes with strings come abilities. Always with strings comes purpose. Lia, for reasons she truly does not know, has all these. Lia is many things, but first and foremost she is a conduit for her god. She is the means by which her god carries out its ambition and it is as natural to her as walking and breathing.

The people of the land have many names and titles for people such as Lia. Yet innocently and without premeditation, they choose not to cast any upon her. Possibly because the circumstances are such that so few are around at the time she is discovered that the word does not spread. Or perhaps they chose not to name her for the same reason the dark ship was without a name.

Now is Marvros' time with Lia. He is given all he needs or wishes. All is explained; however, understanding and awakening are completely up to him. What is before him, truly for the first time, is a choice. No judgment hangs over this decision. No demons are waiting in the shadows. All Marvros has to do is to choose how he wishes to spend his eternity. This is his reward for being called.

Night falls on the hero. Morning will shed light on the man.

4) Dawn

Time is not endless on the *Talon*. For the others, Lia has been hours with Marvros. The sky now red, the water calm, the men exhausted; and still each and every one of them is there on deck when Lia comes back. Fear cannot hold a candle to curiosity. Whatever their beliefs, each man, especially heroes, must learn what they can, when they can, about themselves. Lia's heroes often blame her for their destiny and few rise above that because the alternative is freewill; and that would mean that they themselves are responsible.

In acknowledging their own weakness, the men watch. Unable to understand, they hope to learn. What is about to happen they will never witness again. Heroes are the best of the best, and even they find comfort in knowing that this calling Lia is about to divine, is not for them.

Lia's duties repeat themselves far too often for her liking. All the events so far are from an old and tired plot but with new names and faces. The problem with being mostly human is that even a familiar story still hurts when it ends sadly; and Lia's stories always end sadly.

Unlike her earlier walk to Marvros being one of forgiveness, the others extend respect to this next walk. She does not demand their respect, it is freely offered. This is not a parade, nor is it a procession. It is the execution of her duty, nothing more. Each walk is the same. The final destination is a mystery, but not a surprise. Unlike the countless walks before, she fears she knows where this one will end. Each time the start is difficult and seems to begin without her will. This time is no different, except it starts with tears.

The pace is hers to set. The route is at her discretion. The destination, however, is not of her choosing. Her duty is to go everywhere and allow the end to find her. Everywhere is the battlefield; and today the battlefield is the deck of the *Talon*. She makes the pace a laborious one -- forcing each step. Carefully and deliberately, she places each foot. Her route passes each of the fallen...one last visit with the dead.

Her path is all about the deck. No order to her route, yet no corner unvisited. The walk has been thorough and still to no end. But not quite; she has skillfully avoided one body. Through the process of elimination she has confirmed her fear. Her walk ends with her friend Kemendil's dead hand reaching out from under a cloth and grabbing her ankle.

How was it that mortals categorize destiny? "Damn the gods who find entertainment in the manipulation of man. Why me? I did not ask for this. I do not want this burden. You are not giving me something; you are instead taking something away." Or is it…"The calling is a blessing. A sign that I am worthy of the attention of a greater being. Glory and recognition will befall me and commoners will admire me."

Selfishness is a very natural and powerful emotion, and possibly the hardest to suppress. Lia knew not to develop an attachment with Kemendil, but allowed it to happen anyway. She knew it would only cause her pain. Cause **her** pain. Her redemption from such a selfish feeling is that "her pain" is her knowledge of the greater good that ultimately awaits Kemendil; the same greater good that her lost friend Marvros fulfilled.

Lia kneels beside Kemendil. With her hand on his chest, she revisits the realm in which she just left Marvros. A similar but different realm. One has just begun; the other is about to end. For Kemendil, this is the beginning of the end. Then, suddenly, Kemendil gasps for air; as if having come up from a long stay under water. His body trembles and his hands grab hold of Lia's clothing. She holds him tightly and the two embrace like victims. Soon, Kemendil relaxes and finds comfort in Lia's arms. His eyes cannot hide his search for reason and understanding. With each changing expression, Lia watches as he remembers and begins to draw meaning.

Kemendil is back. He gains control of his eyes and they meet Lia's. Her eyes are wet with sorrow. If she could, she would put everything back. She would put Kemendil back to death. But Kemendil understands, now. He's beginning to see what Lia is all about. And as quickly as it came, it goes. Kemendil loses control and weeps. Tears not for himself, but for his friend. How rare is a friendship when both have come to terms with their own sacrifices, and yet find greater pain in the sacrifices of the other.

The two do not speak for the remainder of their travels at sea. Not for any particular reason. Their bond has not changed. Perhaps it is because their bond remains untouched that the two do not know how to move forward. Kemendil should be, and is, confused. He apparently accepts that. Lia's uncertainty of the situation, however, is a new element in an otherwise predictable eternity; and she is not the least bit comfortable.

5) First light

Immediately upon reaching port and with no ceremony, Kemendil and Lia go their separate ways. The rest of the men are relieved to have made it to the end. They too, know they have witnessed a new beginning. Lia does not know when she will see her friend again. He has to find his own way now, and there is nothing she can do for him. Kemendil must become the hero he has been destined to be. Lia must continue sewing her threads of fate. Working several strands at a time; endlessly bonding them all together like a wound rope.

Her resources do not support her creations; like a seamstress who is expected to make a ballroom gown from patches of material intended for a quilt. She is the conductor of an orchestra with musicians who are unaware of their ability. Lia must direct but not lead, teach but not tell, and most importantly show but not do. Lia is like the mountain. Her vision is clear and straight like a mountain peak, yet her journey is as winding as a mountain stream, twisting and turning in every direction. So frustrating -- seeing the destination but not knowing the route. Her mountain is vast, challenging, demanding, and offers her little rest.

Destiny and eternity are two elements that should never meet. Lia has been caught in this spiral of dual existence for as long as she can remember. Following a path she can never wander too far from, finding herself doing the same things over and over, seeing the end but unable to get there, and often feeling helpless.

Her repeating plot is simple; but like one's favorite bedtime story, each time is something new and fascinating. For Lia, the stakes are high, and she cannot afford herself the luxury of experimentation or mediocrity. This pattern works, and to abandon it would be reckless and irresponsible. So she doesn't.

Or is she unable to? To spend any time pondering the scope of this question will just bring further frustration, yet she has been spending more and more time doing just that. Argued through debate or through war, the wills of all the gods of this world are carried out by two means: attach strings to the man and call it destiny, or attach strings to everything but the man and call it freewill.

Some men entertain such conspiracies; others discard them as folklore. Ironically, knowing the truth makes no difference. God intervention or not; man only has what he is given, and what he is given is often linked to what he offers. In the end, it all comes down to one's attitude and outlook, those being the only things one has any real control over. An eternity of hardship can still weaken even the heartiest of wills, and Lia questions more and more the nature of the strings attached to her. For now, however, the debate does not get the best of her as she finds just enough purpose in her destiny to help her cope with today's beginnings and endings.

Just in time, too. Today is the beginning of another ending.

6) Daybreak

More than thirty years since departing the *Talon* and Lia looks but a day older. A benefit of her particular set of strings. Never far, however, is the other side of duty. Her duty today is to rejoin an old friend. Anybody else would be enjoying the soft green grass and cloudless blue sky. Nature has outdone itself in a bouquet of serenity. The rolling hills and blooming meadows invite imagination and irresponsibility. It is, unfortunately, all wasted on Lia. She stands atop her hill in the middle of nowhere. Today, for her, no other place could be more important.

For a being so connected with human nature, Lia can be remarkably removed. Is she truly unaware of the weight she carries? Or does she embrace it as a reminder of her trespasses? Is she a saint or a demon? Has she forgotten how to recognize the joy life offers, and instead sees only the pain?

A mile away, a form rolls over the crest of a hill; disappearing in a valley and then reappearing and stopping on the next nearer hilltop. It is a band of heroes -- led by Kemendil.

Reunions do not always go well. Regardless of how the hero may set out after receiving The Calling, they often have too much time to think about things. Things that cause men to doubt and fear. Things that create opportunity for undesirable forces to attach and grow. Things that no man should be burdened with. Lia would be deceiving herself to deny she has thought and worried about Kemendil. Of all man's strengths, willpower can be the quickest to fade. She is wise enough not to expect to meet the young man she left back on the ship. However, she is also foolish enough to hope she meets a man that reminds her of an old friend.

A speck breaks away from the band of heroes and moves swiftly down and around the few hills between them and Lia. With each second, Lia learns more about this stranger. He rides without effort, is well armed and armored, and bears the colors of royalty. He is magnificent.

In an apparent moment of weakness, standing on this hilltop, Lia allows a wisp of cool air to free her senses. Still careful not to be overwhelmed, she cannot resist enjoying the sensation of a bit of

pollen.   Her heart, ever waiting for such an
opportunity, rushes her body with hope and
dreams. For now, time slows. Lia sees more and
with greater clarity. Many things previously hidden
now become grand.   The grass, sky, she and
Kemendil all flow together.   She recalls that there
were moments like these in the past; many times in
fact. Yet, she cannot recall the last one.

The moment now over, Lia cannot put off
preparing herself any longer.   Conflict and even
battle can be the dinner dance at some reunions;
enough to be cautious.   Kemendil draws his blade
and keeps it low and to one side of his horse. Lia
remains   still.   Kemendil's   approach   is   the
accumulation of everything destructive, yet his
charge is like a fragile streamer in the wind.

Experience is calling her a fool. Did her heart
choose a poor time to distract her?   She is out of
time and the massive steed is brought to a climactic
stop just feet away!   In one motion, Kemendil
dismounts and charges her! No! He dismounts and
rushes to her.   Blade forward, eye to eye; Kemendil
puts the sword point to the ground, kneels, and
bows. Lia's hand reaches out but stops short. This
man before her is no longer a friend; he is a hero;
and heroes deserve respect; even from a divine
being.

For the first time in a long time, Lia enjoys the grass and sky.

7) Morning

Within just a few days of Lia joining Kemendil's group, they approach the remains of a small village. For the first time, Lia gets a glimpse of the evil this band pursues. The smoke and ash have long settled, but the foul presence and lost innocence still hang in the air. All is blackened from what must have been many incredibly intense and moving infernos. Several charred frameworks and skeletons are all that remain of this village of families. The bodies preserved in place and torment; some with weapons, others running, a few covering the young. Clearly, the villagers had no chance.

The men don't stop. A respectful pace and path through this landmark of evil is taken, and each internalizes the experience. Kemendil watches his men. Lia watches Kemendil. This is not the first of these villages this group has come across. Never found is any evidence that explains why. Some devastated villages found with bodies, some without. Remaining in the hands and in the position of some of the fallen are clues that the people resisted. Hopeless opposition to an overwhelming evil is the greatest testimony to the will of man.

Mortals try to separate heroes and men, but they shouldn't; they are one and the same. They are made from the same ingredients: heart and soul. The only thing that separates Kemendil's men from those of this village is scope. Men teach, sow, and harvest morals and values. Heroes have the responsibility to create the legends and to protect the soil. Hero and man find purpose in the other. The gods did unwittingly give one gift without strings to all the creatures in this playground of theirs; that being passion. When one tries to simplify the mysteries in their lives, like passion, they cannot.

Once clear of the village the team breaks into a run. Each of them has taken something. Each of them has left something behind. What remains unchanged is their shared commitment and the burden of their purpose. The scenery has lost its color and shape. Shades of grey cover the mundane contour of the landscape as they move on.

Eventually over time and one by one, they emerge from this cloaked outlook and allow themselves to enjoy some of life's little pleasures.

Heroes are men, and when they can, they play. They indulge themselves in careless charges and meaningless diversions, allowing a release of unconstructive emotions in exchange for light and vision.

Consciously or not, these men are creating hope. Hope is rooted in faith, and faith in some kind of form is the one common ingredient in all of their passion. Kemendil's men are different from one another in countless ways, but passion is the one thing that they all have in common. Passion tempered with faith is what separates good from evil; and it all starts with hope.

Lia had forgotten about hope. It wasn't until a few days ago, on the hilltop watching Kemendil approach that she began to remember. Of all the strings, and of all the emotions; no one, not even gods, fully understands the power of hope.

Hope is a right for all men. Heroes express their hope and passion in the form of action, and commoners express it through husbandry; and although their roles may be different it is their combined hopes that keep the vision of man true.

Nurturing that symbiotic relationship throughout their years of travel, Kemendil's band has made many friends and allies. Deeds that have gone unrecognized have made them noble. Deeds that have been recognized have made them humble. Barbarian to royalty, sage to commoner, they all have a stake in the events and in the future. A hero speaks all languages when he speaks with his heart. He gains trust and loyalty when he admits to not knowing all the answers, but instead seeks to understand the questions. Kemendil has been listening to many questions.

This evil is far reaching, and it has been fought in small pockets with some victories. The real battle lies with some yet to be discovered entity. What does one call the unknown? Perhaps it is best left without name. The matter need not be named to be known. Everybody knows what needs to be done; and each has come to terms with his role. Although they may deliver the killing blow, the battle does not lie exclusively with the heroes.

Kemendil has spent much of his time building an alliance of men. Much of his troop comes from both royal house and revered clan alike. His team's heart and faith are far more significant than their house and history; for in this company, savage and noble must act as brothers. It is not clear if it is Kemendil's heroes that reflect the structure of the alliance, or the alliance that reflects the heart of the heroes. This question need not ever be resolved. For now it is sufficient to merely recognize its existence. What's important is that this question be remembered and reflected upon later, when all this is over and before the walls of differences are rebuilt.

One constant that Lia has noticed throughout her eternity with heroes is that all heroes come through in the end. Although the time and place for the end of Kemendil's journey she cannot see, it is clear to Lia that this group has already come through much, many times over. To where will this group evolve? Or is the question, to where will they take Lia? A silent call draws their focus. Duty is close.

The heroes stride as one and create a wave of power and pride miles ahead of them. A halo of a soft roar exists about them not unlike a distant thunder that demands respect, yet not fear. For the fortunate onlooker, time seems to slow to allow the person to truly grasp and appreciate the company in which he keeps.

Lia is honored to be in their presence.

8) Midday

Today is beautiful. Kemendil's men only notice after forcing the luxury upon themselves. This task of theirs is big, and it is close, and it is demanding all their energy. Duty wears on even the heartiest of heroes. Recent months have been a constant flood of skirmishes, negotiations, and growing. Still, the team continues. They may think about their journey's end a lot, but they dare not discuss it. To discuss an end in which such sacrifice will be demanded charges a toll against the hope; and hope is a precious partner to be cherished.

Ahead, men are seen working the fields with earnest and purpose. These men have cleared a large portion of the woods, and they must have been at it for quite some time. But it is odd; the clearing goes on in all directions. There are men everywhere. Where is their village and what could they possibly need with all this timber? The men work relentlessly at chopping down the trees. The trees are then collected and secured into large bundles. Little care is taken on preparation. This activity is clearly quantity focused. Not one person is observed resting or talking.

Frequently, women lead teams of beasts to the clearings. Many teams can be seen all about, as logs are then attached. The time together is kept brief. One has to look hard to notice any interaction. Direct contact between the men and women seems to be avoided, and what little personal time they steal, they spend in fear. The women bring food and water to the men and then depart with the fallen trees.

But depart to where? All these people cannot be from one village; and where are the children? The constant chopping and cracking of splintering trunks grows heavy with the heroes. An explanation is not presenting itself and one of Kemendil's men approaches him. Kemendil nods in acceptance of this man's suggestion to take a closer look. Another goes with him.

Using their unique skills, the two move about swiftly and discretely in the direction of the hauled away logs. Passing only a few hills, the landscape quickly becomes barren. There is nothing to be seen in any direction. The two follow and hide in ruts cut deeply from trees dragged behind beasts. They find an area where countless teams and wagons, all dragging trees, converge from all directions like giant ants flowing in and out of a crevice between two large hills.

The activity involves thousands of people and consumes countless tons of wood. The two scouts plan their approach. The source of this evil, their destiny, lies beyond those hills. Plumes of smoke can be seen everywhere. As they crawl over the top of one of these hills, staying under the cover of some craggy rocks, the scouts observe a horrific sight.

This crevice is one of many, surrounding a gash in the ground the size of a small city. Immediately noticed are intermittent streams of flames shooting up from this pit like a fountain of fire. All about are thousands of people from all areas and communities. From stunted dwarves to towering ogres all populate this menagerie. Beings going about laborious activities as any slave would do under tyranny.

Intermixed within the people are beings that can only be described as demons, overseeing all activity in the area. They observe the coming and going of materials, handling and distribution of food, and occasionally remind the population who's in charge. Each entrance to this pit area is watched by several large creatures, each ablaze with flame and receiving regular streams of fire from the pit.

Many of the entrances are busy with teams bringing trees apparently used to fuel this demonic hive; some entrances are not so busy. These streams of fire from the crevice also supply smaller servants with purpose. Activity to one side answers the question regarding the children.

Sectioned off into several small groups and supervised by plenty of the demons, the children are tending animals or working animal hides. The children's close proximity to the roads the women travel is no coincidence. Stripped of all dignity, the people move about as if in a trance. The only feeling they have left, their love for their children, is used to control them. A complete sense of worthlessness has consumed them.

The scouts are stunned with the magnitude of the horror. It is unimaginable. The two are trained observers and are overwhelmed with the input. They have seen many atrocities yet were completely unprepared for this. As carefully as they came, the two men return to the group to describe what they saw.

Not one of Kemendil's men can deny the shock of the two men's report. To what end will the gods play? Certainly Lia's god could have prevented this, yet here it is in all its horror! To remain sane, men must have faith in their gods; but even after countless miracles, Lia wonders. If there is no end, why continue? Is all this a journey and not a destination? If it happens to end does it mean that the gods have given up? Does there come a time when a god tires? What makes all these questions insignificant is the unthinkable alternative.

Faith does not require explanation only passion. The heroes move on. Lia then notices Kemendil appearing to be asking himself these very same questions. She observed only days earlier his wisdom with his friends and allies, and what it takes to be strong and to help others be strong. He sought not the answers, but instead to understand the questions. Is this hero now losing his faith?

Kemendil catches himself lost in thought. His thoughts are most certainly the same as his men's, and he knows he must address the group. This is far worse than any of them ever imagined. What lies ahead he and Lia must do, but no mortal would blame the rest of them for turning back. Kemendil has not lost his faith; in fact his passion and self-sacrifice are ever stronger. But so too is his compassion and love for his men.

Each in turn notices Kemendil's gaze and they become confused. They do not recognize the look on his face; it is unfamiliar to them. They gather as he approaches. He meets them each eye to eye as a proud father would a deserving son. Kemendil has the look of a father who has asked too much of his devoted son, and is ashamed in having let it go so far. He speaks of his old life and of his new life. He speaks of destiny and how important it is to make the best of what you have instead of complaining about what you have not. He tries to put into words an explanation of himself to men who already know him too well.

He extends to them an apology.

Hidden in his message he thanked the men for all their help and sacrifice. And, equally hidden, he asked his men to leave. Hidden as it was, though, nobody missed it. Kemendil was right about his thoughts being their thoughts. All of them had countless questions about everything and certainly the fate before them. What Kemendil overlooked was because they all think as he does, quitting or turning back never occurred to any of them.

Lesser men might have been insulted by the suggestion to leave; but lesser men would not be there now. Scope of duty is one of the things that separates the hero from the man; and right now, on this grassy knoll, there is a band of heroes of epic proportion. The enemy now known and the challenge formally accepted, it is time to meet destiny.

9) Afternoon

Destiny willingly waits for rituals and ceremonies as the men don their armor and colors as they collect at the top of the hill. They internally celebrate their identity and their unity. Each hero giving a settling gaze upon the other. Heroes cut from the same cloth. They take the time now to recognize the commitment and sacrifice of all, because it would not have been appropriate to discuss such things earlier; and because it is most likely they will not be around to do it later.

Some things should never change. Lia believes now that perhaps one of her questions, "*Why* me?" is in fact being answered. Watching these men wanting to be more than they are, to learn and to help others, is perhaps a sign that mankind is growing and that her role is changing. *Maybe* there is something new about all this and as a gift, her god has arranged for her to discover it for herself. *Maybe* it is not the god with the power after all, but instead it is the man; and this is man taking the first step toward accepting that responsibility. *Perhaps* it is not Lia's responsibility to lead, but instead to teach. Guide and help man, not direct him. 'Maybe' and 'Perhaps' are huge leaps from 'Why.'

Perhaps, Lia is ready to be less anonymous. Still, all this is for tomorrow. Today, she still has a destiny to fulfill.

Each man makes final adjustments to his equipment. It was already perfect, but that does not matter. It is a ritual, a meditation process that allows them to focus and become one with their instruments and with each other. It is the drop of water becoming one with the sea. Looking out over the wasteland, some of the heroes plan their attack; some relive past loves and lives; and some enjoy the little pleasures this day is offering. One thing is certain; things will be different tomorrow.

Waiting for destiny can seem like an eternity. One doesn't find it, it finds the one; and it has no appreciation for time. But it does show favor for heroes. It hints of its arrival through the energy that can be felt through the heightened senses; and the heroes know this is the point of no return.

Then, on far off hills, masses can be seen forming on the crests as armies of Kemendil's allies appear. Lia and Kemendil look to one another with shallow smiles and nods. Then, as if responding to a silent horn, the summoned masses glide down the hillsides toward the demon pit. The rows of men charge the fiery compound like a tidal wave and the area billows like water on coals.

With cool determination, Kemendil slowly and purposely directs his horse to the low ground behind the hill. Like a ballet, all the men fall in with even stride and spacing, their actions precise and their motions with purpose. It is with strong mixed emotions that Lia looks on. Never before has such a group of champions come together; and she suspects it will never happen again. And, too, she looks upon this same group as her children; proud and concerned.

Their walk becomes a trot and then a gallop. The individuals become a mass and it charges through the valleys, sending thunder ahead as a warning. For an instant, time slows for Lia and she is given one last chance to see her friends; her heroes. But this time, it is her heart that sees clearly. Her eyes see the flowing colors and powerful bodies in command of their tools of destruction. But it is her heart that bonds her to them. It is what makes her who she is and allows her to feel the pride they feel.

Given to her is a calm before the storm; a peace within conflict through which she can influence and operate. This is her gift to them; a second pair of eyes, a steady hand, a fighting chance that will stay with them until the end. For the moment, this gift works the other way; giving peace and courage back to Lia.

Then it begins.

Fire creatures at this crevice are caught surprised by the charging party. Most of them had been directed to fend off the attacking armies. Surprised, but no less lethal, the demon creatures attack back with weapons of flame and abilities to weaken the heroes' wills. This skirmish is quick and deadly, but now the team's element of surprise has vanished. Lia and Kemendil's men are not the only force with a bond. Whatever lies in that pit apparently is keenly aware of their presence, as noticed by all the minions and demons now looking their way.

Now inside the compound, with the hell pit within sight, the heroes realize the scouts' description was mild. This was a demonic meat house with unthinkable atrocities. People no longer useful for labor became subjects of experimentation or pleasure. This being what they notice up here, they dare not think about what awaits them at their destination...the pit. No time to think; only time to act. The forces of evil are upon them as they make their way to the passages below.

Some stay back at the entrance to hold off the converging force. Time is about to be bought and the others know it is up to them to honor their sacrifice. They continue down into the bowels of this fissure of evil. The heat is unbearable and the fire bites at them at every turn. Lia remains up top with those who stayed behind. Her powers allow her to provide some relief from the heat to those below as she revitalizes the heroes above.

Knowing one's death is at hand, a hero seizes the moment. Like a candle receiving a puff of breath, the hero flairs up in an instant of glory before being snuffed out. Their moment of glory is now; and with the skill of an artist and the will of a fool, they take each moment with purpose and with love for life. Each second is an extension on an expired lease. For them, there could be no better way to die. Here, now, together, and for the others.

With the price of time having been paid; below, Lia finds the others scattered about in a maze of bridges and landings amongst a lake of lava and streams of fire. The demon horde she left above is only minutes away and the obvious target of the attack is seemingly unscathed. To see more clearly, she closes her eyes and opens her heart.

Servants of evil continue to climb up out of the liquid fire, and demons seem to crawl out from a fire portal being held open by what can only be described as an enormous embodiment of lava in the form of a demon. Fire is its skin and lava is its flesh, and it appears to be under the control of something not yet seen. Hell is making its way to the surface.

Having made his way near the portal, a wizard hero draws every ounce of energy he can and transforms himself into a body of water. The water draws all the heat from the platform and the sudden shock cracks the stone. It is felt throughout the pit and sends shock waves in all directions.

For an instant, the fire portal shuts and a pair of orange eyes can be seen from within rock near Kemendil. Through their bond, the team is focused and instantly knows what must be done and they all act as one.

The weakened stone platform cannot hold any longer and fails. The portal and the demon holding it open fall into the lava lake, and the protective stone wall concealing the lesser devil weakens. The heroes attack the now vulnerable source; stopping and eventually reversing the demonic flow. Victory is theirs!

10) Dusk

Back above ground and having tended the last of the injured, Lia knows all too well her next task. This time, however, it is no walk of forgiveness; it is a walk of pride. Pride in the survivors, the fallen, and in her. She approaches Kemendil's still body and kneels beside her old friend. Now will be Kemendil's time with Lia and he will be given all the time he needs or wishes. But as she reaches for him, his hand swings up and grabs her arm!

Lia knows Kemendil was dead when he was carried out from the collapsing pit. The heroes are always dead! Yet his eyes are now bright and they focus on hers. His mouth forms a smile and opens to allow a breath to enter his chest. He pulls her to him and whispers into her ear.

Slowly pulling back, Lia first has a puzzled expression, but then concentrates for a moment. She briefly looks away and then back to Kemendil's waiting eyes, and replies, "Yes. Yes, I do hear it." Kemendil smiles one last time...and then dies. Lia takes control of eternity, drawing it out to savor her friend's message. A message she never previously considered yet makes everything meaningful again!

Leaving the world behind and with a new glow, Lia follows through with her divine duty to prepare the hero for his eternity. This place and time of transition to the afterworld in which they now meet is no surprise to Kemendil. Of course he had no knowledge of it, but he did somehow know that it was waiting for him. One last time together, the two spend most of it discussing and sharing insight into the questions. Eventually, Kemendil chooses how he will spend his eternity and accepts his reward.

For a while longer, Lia stays and reflects. Destiny can, and has, waited for her before; it can wait a bit longer now. She thinks about what it is she does for her god; her duty to carry out his will. She, too, thinks about how she wished for it to end; that it is sometimes too much. Now, she is not so sure. She is finding a new hope and strength in the message left with her by her friend. Night falls on the hero Kemendil. Morning will certainly shed new light on Lia.

Lia never understood how or why she was chosen to serve her god. A good amount of her time recently has been spent questioning her god's will and the actions of the other gods. Lia believes she is now ready to move on. Perhaps it is time for the people to give her a name. Lia returns to the wasteland and finds herself holding Kemendil's body. She carefully puts him to rest and offers her final respects.

Now, her final duty of this particular day of eternity awaits her. It is time for the chosen one to find her. She stands and slowly turns in a circle. Stretching out her arms, she embraces the day. The walk this time does not seem to be dreaded like the others before it. With Kemendil's final question and message ever strong on her mind, she goes over it and over it.

So much has been new to her this time that she wants to be careful not to forget any of it. Everything was special and to hurry would lessen it. She begins her walk with a light and sure step. The following steps are swift and delicate as though she were dancing. Her heart is gay and, for the first time, she truly understands what all this is about. She now hears what has always been there yet had never heard before...before Kemendil had pointed it out to her.

Filling the air all around her are the sounds of celebration! From over the hills and from every man and from every child is cheering and joy!

Filling every void and bridging every gap is laughter and rejoicing for returned loved ones and a returned life. This is not just about or for the heroes. This is for all men -- including her; and Lia realizes that she has been deaf to the meaning all along.

She has always been careful not to pretend to be the hero. 'They' are the heroes. But not anymore. Today, tomorrow, and from now on, Lia will accept her role in destiny and her place in the world. Lia once again has hope; and instead of searching for answers, she now seeks to understand the questions. She has accepted that she is in fact a hero...because her son has told her so.

ISBN 142518794-3